Diana Dances

By Luciano Lozano

annick press
toronto + berkeley

To Fernando
– Luciano Lozano

"Good morning!" Diana's teacher greeted the students one Monday when they got to class. "Today we'll be preparing for your math test."

Diana did not like to study. But above all, she did not like math.

Diana was bored at school,
and never got good grades.

And then, at home Monday afternoon, Diana's mother got more bad news from the school. It said Diana would fail if she could not learn her multiplication tables!

So Diana's mother decided to hire a private teacher.

But Diana could not concentrate.

"What's wrong with Diana?"
Her mother worried. She took
Diana to the doctor, but the
doctor found nothing wrong. She
suggested Diana see a different kind
of doctor, called a psychologist.

Diana didn't think she had a
problem. So why did everyone else?

She left feeling confused and sad.

Diana and her mother went to see the
psychologist, determined to find a solution.

This new doctor
observed, and he listened,
then he approached Diana and said:

"I'm going to talk with your mother
for a moment. Wait for us here."

Before leaving, he turned on
the radio, and left the room
wrapped in a soft melody.

For a moment, Diana forgot where she was.
She smiled and closed her eyes as her body moved
gracefully, following the rhythm of the music.

Diana's mother watched from the doorway. She had never seen her daughter move like that before! The psychologist coughed a little, then declared:

"Madam, your daughter is not sick! Your daughter is a dancer! I recommend taking her to dance school!"

Am I a dancer? thought Diana. *I'm a dancer!*

At dance school, there were many girls and boys who did not stop moving. Just like Diana.

She could hardly wait to join all the other children.

Diana felt like she was
floating off the ground.
Everyone smiled.
Nobody needed to talk.
Diana was so happy.

She spent the whole week waiting for
her next dance class.

She practiced every day at home while reciting her multiplication tables.

She discovered that it was easier for her to think if she was moving.

Diana even started to have a good time at school.

"Twenty-seven!" Diana yelled,
when the teacher asked for an
answer to nine times three.

And at night, Diana
dreamed that she danced
and danced, repeating
her favorite dance steps
over and over.

Maybe, Diana thought, she would get to
dance in a big theater someday.

Maybe not.

But she would never stop dancing.

And of course,
she passed her math test.

Annick Press edition, 2019
Translated by Yanitzia Canetti, Cambridge BrickHouse, Inc.
English translation edited by Annick Press
Cover design for Annick Press edition by Alexandra Niit

Cataloging in Publication

Lozano, Luciano, 1969-
[Bea baila. English]
    Diana dances / Luciano Lozano.

Translation of: Bea baila.
ISBN 978-1-77321-248-7 (hardcover).--ISBN 978-1-77321-247-0 (softcover)

    I. Title. II. Title: Bea baila. English.

PZ7.L96764D53 2019   j813'.6   C2018-903726-1

Published in the U.S.A. by Annick Press (U.S.) Ltd.
Distributed in Canada by University of Toronto Press.
Distributed in the U.S.A. by Publishers Group West.

Printed in China

www.annickpress.com
www.ilustrista.com

Also available as an e-book.
Please visit www.annickpress.com/ebooks.html
for more details.

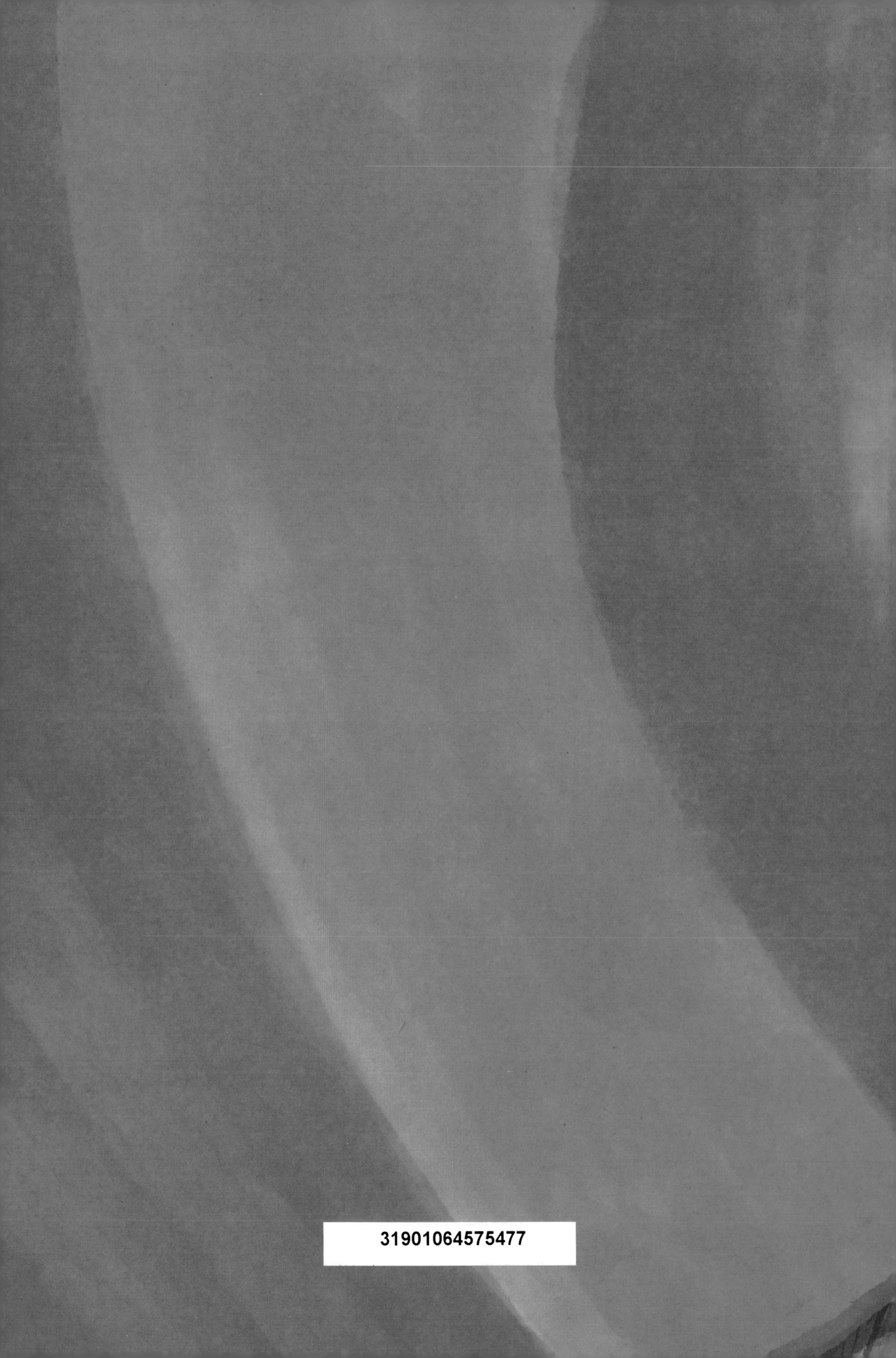